Tonight I will be sharing with you some of my favorite **scary stories.**

Stories so *creepy,*

so **terrifying**...you may have trouble sleeping.

So if you are the kind of person who hears bumps in the night or

who **dreads** putting a hand over the *edge* of the bed...

I suggest you read no further.

First published in the United States of America in 1997 by
Walker Publishing Company, Inc.

Published simultaneously in Canada by
Thomas Allen & Son Canada, Limited, Markham, Ontario

Library of Congress Cataloging-in-Publication Data
O'Malley, Kevin, 1961-
    Velcome / written and illustrated by Kevin O'Malley.
      p.    cm.
    Summary: An illustrated collection of scary stories with humorous endings, featuring
    such elements as a boy being followed home by a coffin, a rapping noise in a haunted
    house, and strange intruders at the front door.
      ISBN 0-8027-8628-6 (hardcover). – ISBN 0-8027-8629-4 (reinforced)
      1. Horror tales, American.  2. Humorous stories, American.  3. Children's
    stories, American. [1. Horror stories. 2. Humorous stories. 3. Short stories.]
    I. Title.
    PZ7.O526Ve  1997
    [E] –dc21

Book design by Shoot the Moon, Inc.

Printed in Hong Kong

10 9 8 7 6 5 4 3 2 1

WARNING!!!
This is the most
intelligent part
of this whole book.

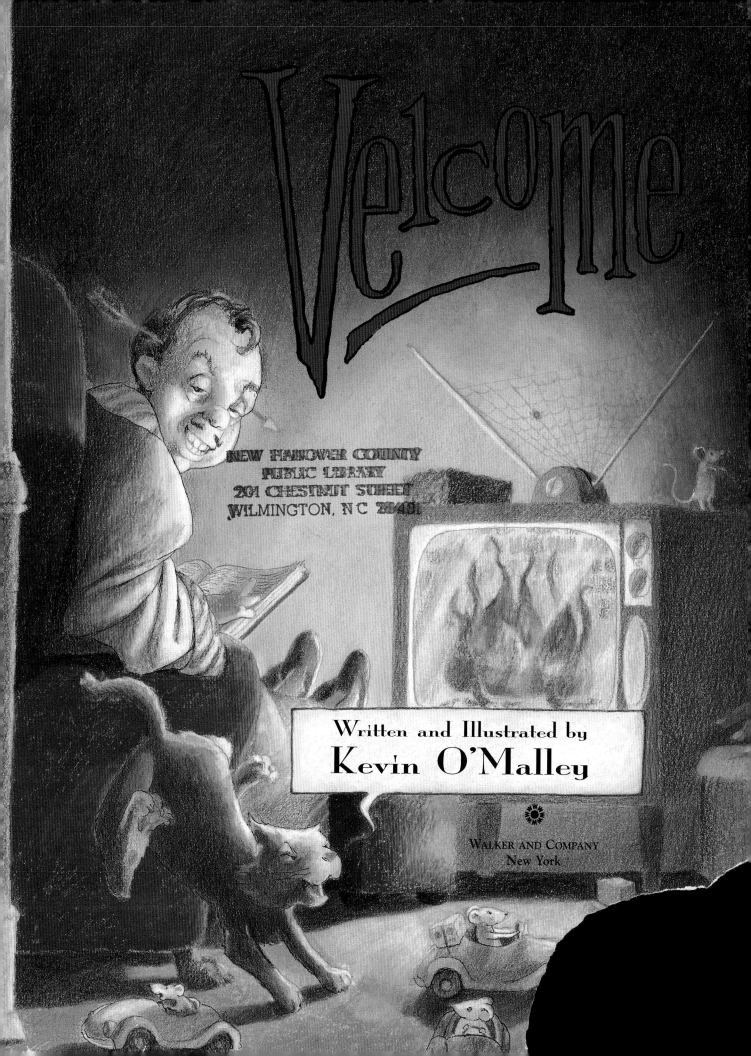

# Velcome

Written and Illustrated by
## Kevin O'Malley

WALKER AND COMPANY
New York

$O$ur first story takes place in a quiet little village
not far from where YOU live.  A young man, very much like
yourself, was returning from soccer practice one evening. A fall wind was
whipping through the trees. It seemed to call the boy's name: "Fred-die...Fred-die,

FRED-die, FRED-Die, FRED-Die, FRED-Die,

**FRED-DIE!"**

As Freddie walked home he passed a graveyard.
A cold chill ran down his spine.

Suddenly Freddie heard a bumping sound behind him.
He turned to see a coffin following him up the road.
Freddie walked a little *faster*.

The coffin bumped a little faster.

Freddie started to **run** ...

the coffin followed, getting closer and closer!

Freddie **raced** to his house and slammed the door behind him.

He could hear the **coffin** bumping at the door.

The bumping got louder and LOUDER until suddenly...

the coffin came crashing through the door.

Freddie **raced** up the steps...

the coffin went bumping along right after him...

What would Freddie do?

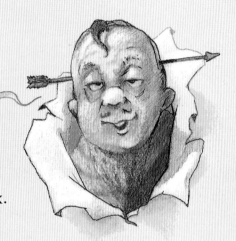

He ran to his room

and got a SMALL box.

He **raced** back to the stairs.

The coffin got closer...

and *closer!*

Freddie took a cough drop out

of the box and threw it at

the coffin

and...

t h e  c o f f i n  s t o p p e d .

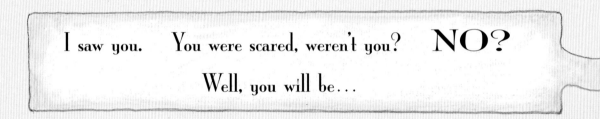
I saw you.    You were scared, weren't you?    NO?

Well, you will be...

There was a young girl **alone** in her apartment. She was *supposed* to be doing her CHORES but instead she was watching T.V.

### Suddenly the phone rang.

"HELLO," she said.

"I am the Viper. I'm coming **up**," said the voice.

Quickly the girl hung up the phone.

A few moments later the phone rang again.

"I am the Viper. I'm coming **up**," said the voice.

The young girl was more than a little worried. She decided not to answer the phone again. When the telephone rang for the ***third*** time she let the answering machine pick it up.

"I am the Viper. I'm coming **up**. I'm almost **there**," said the voice.

The young girl was positively **terrified**.

The moment the caller hung up, she called the police.

"He says he's the ***viper*** and he's coming **up**," she sobbed.

Shall I go on?  Maybe you're too *scared*?  No?  O k a y . . .

Suddenly there was a
# knock
at the door.

Slowly she turned the doorknob… S-l-o-w-l-y she opened the door…

There was a little man with a *bucket* in his hand.

The young girl

Sssscccreeeeaaaaamed!

And the little man said…

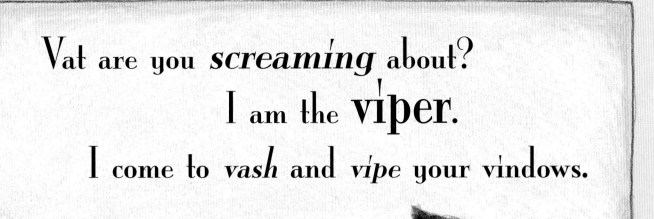

Vat are you *screaming* about?
I am the **viper**.
I come to *vash* and *vipe* your vindows.

I'm trying to "Vipe" this whole thing from my BRAIN!

Why don't we take a little break? I know how **terrified** you must be.

Maybe you need a little warm milk to CALM yourself down.

I will entertain you with some scary jokes.

Mommy, Mommy, can I play with little brother?
Absolutely not! You've already dug him up three times this week.

Mommy, Mommy, what's a vampire?
Just eat your blood, dear, before it clots.

What's grosser than gross?
Eating a bowl of rice and the last piece **crawls** out.

This

one

I call . . .

On the edge of town, there was a **house**.

A **haunted** house.

People *tried* to live there.

But the rapping, rapping, **RAPPING** sound that came from the house

drove

them

*crazy*.

One day a boy came to live in the haunted house. He heard the

rapping, rapping, **RAPPING**.

He followed the sound.

Up the stairs... around the corner... down the hall... into his room.

The rapping got louder and louder and LOUDER.

Slowly he opened the closet door and...

He found a roll
of brown

Brown wrapping paper. Now *that* was scary.

Wouldn't you agree? You're laughing?

Well, we will just see how **much** you laugh at what

I'm about to show you.

This picture is so horrible...

you had better call your mommy.

A plate of
mixed

vegetables!!!

Now that I've scared you out of your pants...
I will scare you out of your skin with this...

# REPORT CARD

English

Math

Science

History

Gym

F-

F

F+

F

F-

F

Have your parents sign this report card and return it to the teacher

Parent sign here

SLAYUM ELEMENTARY

# Your report card!

**Finally** I will tell you a story so *terrible*...so HORRIBLE, you won't be able to sleep tonight. It's called the *Didja*.

The rain poured down like hammers and the lightning made strange shapes and shadows.

Then she heard a sound. *Quiet at first*, then louder.

Knock knock.

She was alone. All alone.

The sound of the storm shook her house, the *lightning* lit up the sky.

"*Who is it?*" she whispered.

But there was no answer.

She was alone. All alone.
And curled up on the couch when *suddenly*, KA-BOOM!

All the lights went out.

The wind *whipped* the trees, and the branches cracked against her house.

Then she heard it *again*.

She was alone.

All alone,

in the **dark**.

Knock knock.

Someone—or something—was at the door.

She pulled herself from the couch.
Her knees quaked.
"*Who is it?*" she asked.

**"Didja,"** said a voice all *drippy* and **deep**.

"Didja what?" asked the girl, her voice just above a whisper.

But there was no answer.

She was *alone*. All alone . . . and the sound of the
wind was driving her mad, *mad*, MAD.
When she heard it again.

Knock knock.

"Who's **there?**" she screamed.

**"Didja,"** called the voice.

"Didja who?" she asked, her voice wracked with terror.

And then in a **deep** and booming voice she heard a reply
that she would never forget as long as she lived . . .

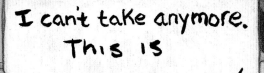